This book belongs to:

....

....

*For Chloe and Ben, too grown up to hold
my hand now, but you will hold my heart forever x – H. H.*

*For my Dad, thank you for holding my hand
and keeping me safe – D. H.*

Editor: Alexandra Koken
Designer: Verity Clark

Copyright © QED Publishing 2013

First published in the UK in 2013 by QED Publishing
A Quarto Group company, 230 City Road, London EC1V 2TT

www.qed-publishing.co.uk

A catalogue record for this book is available from the British Library.

ISBN 978 1 78171 128 6

Printed in China

The Otter Who Loved to Hold Hands

Heidi *and* Daniel Howarth

QED Publishing

Every night, when they go to sleep, Otto's family hold hands so they don't drift apart. And every morning, when they wake up, they all let go again.

Except for little Otto . . .

Otto worried about swimming.
He worried about diving and he
worried about getting lost.

But most of all, he worried
about being alone.

Every morning, Mum said,
"Please let go, Otto. I can't do
anything with you holding
my hand!"

But Otto shook his head.
He didn't want to let go.

"I can't swim on my own!"
he squealed, clinging on to Mum.

He knew he would float –
but letting go was still scary.

What if he drifted
out to sea?

"You can do it," Mum said gently.
But Otto shook his head.
He didn't want to let go.

The other cubs enjoyed
playing, chasing and splashing.

Otto wanted to join in,
but he just couldn't let
go of Mum and Dad.

"Go and play," said Dad. "I'll watch you from here."

But Otto shook his head.
He didn't want to let go.
"I'm scared!" Otto cried.

"Don't let go!" Otto begged, as Mum
tried to open an oyster shell.

"I'm still right here," Mum sighed.
But Otto just had to hold on.

Mum and the shell bobbed and
rocked as Otto clung to her.

When Mum finally opened the oyster shell, Otto saw a beautiful shiny pearl gleaming inside it.

"It's amazing," Otto said. "Ooh, look! There's an otter inside, just like me!"

Otto reached out to the little otter in
the pearl and before he knew it . . .

... he was holding the beautiful pearl in both his hands.

Otto saw a happy otter
floating all by himself . . .

. . .and realized
it was
him!

"We're so proud of you!" Mum said.
"Well done, Otto!" Dad said.

"I let go!" Otto cried. "I'm floating
on my own and I'm fine!"

"Hooray! Come and play with us!"
called the other little otters.

So now, every day,
Otto **splashes**

and **swims**

and **plays**
with his friends.

He's a very **happy** little Otter.

But he still looks forward to night-time,
when he and his family hold hands as
they drift off to sleep.

Next steps

After reading the book, have another look at the cover. Do the children think Otto looks happy? Do they think he will feel happier now that he doesn't have to hold hands all the time?

Why do the children think Otto loved to hold hands? Did they find it hard to let go of their Mum or Dad's hand when they were little? What would they say to a friend or younger sibling who's afraid to let go?

When Otto sees his mum open a shell with something special inside it, he is curious and wants to have a closer look. Discuss what it means to be curious and to want to find out more about something. Do the children have something they feel curious about? What is their favourite subject at school and does it make them want to learn more?

Trying new things can be scary. Otto is afraid to swim and play with the other little otters, even though it looks like fun. Were the children ever afraid of trying something new, like swimming or riding a bicycle? How did they overcome their fears?

Ask the children to act out the story. One child could play Otto, and the others could be the rest of his family and friends. When the otters sleep and hold hands the children could all lie down on the floor and hold hands. Can they make up a song to show how happy Otto is once he learns to let go?